LAND OF DEATH

ERIC S BROWN AND ALEX LAYBOURNE

Severed Press
Hobart Tasmania

LAND OF DEATH

Copyright © 2015 by Eric S Brown & Alex Laybourne
Copyright © 2015 by Severed Press

www.severedpress.com

All rights reserved. No part of this book may be reproduced or transmitted in any form or by any electronic or mechanical means, including photocopying, recording or by any information and retrieval system, without the written permission of the publisher and author, except where permitted by law.
This novel is a work of fiction. Names, characters, places and incidents are the product of the author's imagination, or are used fictitiously. Any resemblance to actual events, locales or persons, living or dead, is purely coincidental.

ISBN: 978-1-925342-24-6

All rights reserved.

LAND OF DEATH

Steve kept the jeep's gas pedal floored. Henry cowered in the passenger seat beside him. Robbins somehow managed not only to stay on his feet in the rear of the jeep, but also to return fire at their pursuers with the vehicle's mounted .50 caliber gun. The sound of the blazing gun drowned out that of the jeep's straining engine. Spent casings flew from the .50 caliber. One of them somehow bounced and landed on Henry who gave a cry of pain as the hot metal stung the back of his neck. His hand swatted at the already gone casing, nearly causing him to lose his hold and go flying out of the jeep. Steve shot out a hand, jerking him into his seat again by the top of the Kevlar vest he wore.

Seeing that Henry was okay, Steve risked a glance to his left and then to his right. He saw that the other surviving two jeeps that had escaped the attack on the base were still with him. All three were being chased by close to a dozen various vehicles ranging from beat up trucks to what passed for military jeeps in this part of the world.

Bullets whizzed and whined by Steve as he drove. He had been in "car chases" before but never anything like this one. It was as if the whole IXAS terrorist group had mobilized and was coming after them. That wouldn't be too far from the truth. The amount of firepower and organization required to hit the base as hard and fast as they had this morning was staggering. No one in command would have ever thought such an attack possible and now they were paying the price for it.

"Steve!" Henry shouted, pointing at something ahead of the jeep.

Steve jerked his head around to look towards the horizon, only the horizon wasn't there anymore. Instead, a cloud of raging sand that stretched towards the heavens had taken its place. The sandstorm had come out of nowhere. Easily miles long across its front, Steve knew there was no hope of dodging it. He didn't dare slam on the brakes. At the speed they were traveling, it would be suicide to try to come to an immediate halt, much less turn around. *On the upside,* Steve thought, *even if those IXAS maniacs are crazy enough to follow in there, we'll be able to lose them for sure....assuming we make it through that thing alive.*

"Hold on!" Steve ordered as the jeep sped onward towards the fury of nature that lay ahead of it.

Steve reached back to pat Robbins' leg, because he doubted the big man had heard him.

"Holy…" Robbins shouted and the .50 caliber fell silent as he ducked and dropped down as best he could behind the jeep's seats.

Then the world around became nothing more than a whirling mass of sand and the screaming of the wind.

****

Steve awoke to pain stabbing through his body. His ribs felt as if someone had smashed a sledgehammer into the dead center of them. The world was a blur as he opened his eyes. He shook his head to clear it as his vision came into focus. The hood of the jeep was folded inward where it wrapped around the base of a large tree. The air was still hot but no longer dry. It was so humid his clothes stuck tightly to his skin. The sea of sand had become a jungle of lush, green foliage.

Rubbing the back of his neck, Steve looked around. He coughed and his ribs exploded with pain. Nothing broken, he knew that much, but if those IXAS crazies had been foolish enough to follow them through the storm, he would not be in much of a position to fight.

"Steve?" A voice called out. It sounded muffled, drowned out by distance. "Steve?" The voice called again. Clearer now, closer. Steve turned his whole body toward the sound. Aches, rather than pain greeted him. Other than the blow to his ribs, he seemed in working order.

"Robbins?" Steve answered, and with a pop that made him wince, his ears cleared and the sounds returned to his world. He heard the hissing of his jeep, and the slow drip of engine fluid, leaking from the fatal wound to the vehicle's undercarriage.

"I'm here. What on earth was that back there?" Robbins called. He appeared suddenly from the other side of the jeep. He had a nasty wound on his head, which had sent a wave of deep crimson down one side of his face. Robbins wiped it away without giving his bloodstained hand a second glance. "Where are the others?" He asked, moving carefully as if he were dizzy and trying to stay on his feet.

Steve looked around. He heard Robbin's question, but his mind was busy working on a different problem. *Where were they all?*

"What happened to the desert?" Henry asked. He was still in the jeep. He had thrown himself to the floor just before the vehicle came to its sudden halt.

Steve opened his mouth to answer, when the annoyingly familiar rattle of gunfire rang out. The three men threw themselves to the floor, and crawled together behind the jeep. Steve gritted his teeth against the pain in his chest.

"Where is it coming from?" Henry asked, as the burst rang out. It was followed by a sound like thunder. A tree fell, crashing through its neighbours. A second, shorter burst of gunfire came.

Steve moved into a crouch and peered around the jeep. He scanned the scene, noticing that even behind them, all traces of the desert and the pursuing terrorist group were gone. The jungle surrounded them. The path their jeeps took could be seen going a few hundred yards through the foliage, only to be swallowed up by the trees. He saw the two other jeeps, one of which was in a similar condition to his own, wrecked beyond use.

The third had missed the trees and come to a stop a hundred yards ahead of them, on the edge of a small clearing.

"Tank, Tank, what do you see?" Steve hissed, at the large man standing behind the mounted .50 calibre machine gun.

Tank raised his arm and without looking back, indicated the direction the gunfire came from and told them to hold their position.

"What is it?" Henry asked, with his voice filled with fear. All of them were disoriented from the crash and their sudden change in location.

"Wait here," Steve said as he pushed away from the jeep, grabbing his M-16 from the back in the process, and moving forward to where Tank stood.

The dash to the third jeep was a short one, but fire burned in Steve's chest by the time he got there. Pulling himself into the back, he stood beside Tank, who stood stiffly, staring across the clearing.

"Is it Lawrence or Abbott?" Steve asked. He could recognize the sound of the US Military rifle. It had a far crisper sound to it than the rifles the IXAS had been using.

Tank shrugged, "Not sure, I've not seen either one since the sand storm died," Tank answered, accepting their change in location as if it were just another day on the job. Tank was a soft spoken, giant of a man. Closer to two meters tall and as wide as any human being Steve had ever known. Tank was a country boy, through and through, born and raised on a farm in South Dakota.

They didn't need to wait long for their answer. A figure burst through the trees and into the clearing. He was running at a hurried pace.

"Abbott," Tank said to Steve. Chris Abbott was an easy man to distinguish, even from a distance. He was almost as tall as Tank was, but as thin as a rake. He bounced along with gangly strides that looked uncoordinated, yet he was the fastest of all of them.

Moving into position, Tank crouched down behind the gun and prepared to fire. Whatever was chasing Abbott was coming their way.

The trees parted and an animal burst into view.

"What the..." Steve began, but his words were silenced by a burst of fire from the mounted weapon. Shots rang out and the stationary vehicle shook from side to side from the recoil of the gun.

Staring across the field, Steve saw a puff of red mist as several shots found their mark, but the creature, whatever it was, would not be stopped. The thing closed the gap on Abbott, who tripped and fell on the jungle floor.

The creature lashed out. Abbott's scream cut above the sound of the second volley of shots that Tank sent in its direction.

This time, the result was definite. Round after round filled the creature's body and with a final, piercing growl, it dropped to the floor. Steve was out of the truck in a flash, ignoring his pain. Tank was not far behind him, with Robbins and Henry a short distance behind them.

Robbins and Henry moved slower, their rifles raised, scanning the perimeter of the clearing. They had not seen the creature that attacked Abbott, but from the amount of fire it took to stop it, they anticipated that there was more trouble out there, waiting for them to run into its path.

"That's a bloody dinosaur!" Tank spoke, shocked. He stood staring at the blood-drenched carcass.

"Don't be a fool, Tank," Steve answered. He had turned his attention to Abbott, ignoring the creature that had attacked him. It was too late, however. Abbot was dead. The creature had eviscerated him in a single swipe. A single gash ran along Abbott's stomach, and his intestines had spilled out onto the grass beside him. Even the Kevlar vest that Abbott wore had not stood a chance against the razor sharp talons.

"Look at it." Tank took a step back. "Look." He grabbed Steve by the shirt and pulled him to his feet. "Tell me what that is!" Tank cried, losing his grip, while he held Steve in a vice-like grip, as his large form trembled.

Steve did look at the creature. Standing up, it would have reached a height of nearly eight feet tall. Its arms were short and curved. Its fingers ended in razor sharp claws. Somehow, the thing reminded Steve more of a bird than a lizard, though there was no question that the thing was reptilian in nature.

"Holy..." Steve breathed knowing Tank was right but still not wanting to admit it.

"Retreat!" The cry went up behind them. "Get out of there. NOW!" Robbins screamed. Robbins' voice was filled with real terror and not at all with the professionalism and cool air of detachment of an experienced soldier.

Without looking, Tank and Steve ran back towards the others, crossing the clearing that seemed to extend a lot further on the retreat than it did during their advance. Behind them, the ground shook and a series of roars rang out like mortar fire.

The men made it to the trees and to the jeep. Only then, when crouched behind their vehicles, surrounded by the familiar smell of oil and grease, did they look back at the scene they had left.

Three more creatures stood in the clearing, having emerged from the same direction as Abbott. They stood by their fallen mate and sniffed the ground. Everybody saw what they were, but none wanted to say it. Even to admit it would mean risking the loss of the small bit of control they still had.

Nobody moved, but all of them watched, horrified as one of the creatures bent down, and tore away a portion of Abbot's body with its jaws. Biting down, it swallowed the meat of the dead soldier greedily, giving a hungry growl as soon as it swallowed the mouthful it had.

"We need to get out of here," Henry whispered. His voice sounded as if he were close to tears. Steve didn't look at him. He couldn't take his eyes from the animals standing before him.

"Those things are… I told you … it's a…" Tank stammered, his mind tumbling.

"They're frigging dinosaurs!" Robbins answered. He still held his rifle at arms, and was crouched down, ready to open fire on the creatures. "They're real life, living, breathing dinosaurs." He stared at the creatures, who had finished what was left of Abbot and they were now circling their fallen mate.

"We should move. We need to get out of here. Back to the desert. I'd rather have terrorists shooting at me, than I would this," Henry whispered. He had pulled a few handguns from the back of the jeep, and slung two additional rifles over his shoulder.

"This can't be real," Tank muttered. He rose to his feet and stepped out into the open.

"Get back here, man," Steve growled, reaching up and pulling his brother in arms back behind the jeep. The large man was limp, heavy and unresponsive. Tank fell against the vehicle with a thud.

In the clearing, the dinosaurs stopped their pacing, and all of the men by the jeep held their breath. One stood up straight, its massive frame extending to full height. It gave a low growl and barked into the air; a series of four sharp, cough-like barks. This was answered a short time later by another, more distant response. The three dinosaurs turned and moved back into the trees, heading back the way they had come.

The group of soldiers remained where they were. Bodies caked in sweat, none wanted to be the first to speak. The jungle absorbed the sound of the dinosaurs' passage, and slowly came to life around them.

"We should move," Robbins offered.

"Where would we go?" Henry asked.

"Anywhere but here. We get back into the jeep, drive the way we came and find the desert again,"

Robbins said. It sounded so simple.

"But we only have one functional jeep, right? I know mine ain't going anywhere, and that one," Steve pointed, "don't look much better. The ones that are left can't carry us all."

"Even if we had more, I don't think we are going anywhere fast," a voice called out and then a face appeared from behind the second wrecked jeep. A young soldier stood up, his face pale, and slicked with sweat. He looked exhausted.

"Watson. Good grief, man, I thought you were a goner," Steve spoke. Wincing as the pain in his chest exploded once more.

"I'm here with Jones, but he's hurt. Hurt bad. There's no way we can move him," the young soldier spoke. There was an empty and sad look to his eyes.

"Stay there," Steve called. "Tank, come with me." He nudged the big guy with his elbow, but Tank gave no response. "Come on, man. Pull yourself together. We're soldiers not babies. We fight what we can see. We are here now, wherever the heck that might be, and we need to survive." Steve was addressing the group now. "We are going to re-group, find a place to make camp and figure out exactly where we are. Now move it, soldiers." The men rallied. Looking at Steve, who had risen to his feet, and stood defiantly, with his rifle across his chest.

"At least that tourniquet has stopped the blood flow some," Robbins said, as they stood behind the second vehicle. Jones lay on the ground. His right leg was broken, the white of bone protruding through his flesh and the blood soaked cloth of his pants. It was clear that Watson had already attempted to splint Jones' leg, after tying the tourniquet that was keeping Jones alive, but even so, strands of flesh hung from the jagged shards of the bone that was visible.

"Tank, we need to get him up and into the back of the jeep and then we need to get moving. Staying here with those things out there is suicide. There's no telling when they'll decide to come back for more." Steve ordered, "Robbins, I want you and Henry on watch. Watson, you get behind the .50 cal. If anything comes through those trees, we take it down."

Steve stopped talking and wiped the sweat from his forehead. "Tank, you got the keys for the jeep?" Steve asked. Tank grinned and tossed a small silver key to Steve.

"Let's do this." Tank nodded his head.

"Everybody, grab as many supplies as you can from the other two jeeps. Henry, see about getting one of those .50 cals from the others jeeps. I have a feeling we may need it. Everyone be prepared to move out on my signal. Robbins, Henry, you hold position until I give the word, got it?" Steve pulled two more M-16s from the back of the broken jeep, handing them out, and then as an afterthought stuffed a few extra magazines into the pockets of his pants. "Alright, let's get to it."

Steve tossed the extra weapons he carried into the last functional jeep and then slid into its driver's seat. Its engine fired up on the first try. Steve drove it at a pace the others could match while walking along beside it. Tank sat in the jeep's rear with Watson standing over him and Jones sprawled out in his lap. Jones' moaning turned to outright shrieks as the jeep bounced along. Tank shoved a spare magazine into Jones' mouth to stifle his screams. Jones' teeth bit down on it hard, his face a twisted grimace of pain.

"Everybody, eyes forward and stay sharp," Steve ordered. "Except for you, Watson. You be ready to blast apart anything that comes up on us from the rear."

The group had barely gotten moving when Robbins jogged up to Steve and asked, "Where's Lawrence?"

"What?" Steve snapped.

"I haven't seen Lawrence since our jeeps hit the sand storm." Robbins was breathing heavily as he spoke. The heat combined with their heavy combat gear was a dangerous combination, even for someone as tough as he was.

"Tank, did you see Lawrence at all?" Steve slowed the jeep as he turned in his seat to glance at the big man.

Tank nodded. "He had hit his head pretty bad. He was pretty messed up and confused. Abbott had gone out into the trees after him when everything hit the fan. I'd wager he's dead given what those things did to Abbott. There's no way Lawrence could have survived against them on his own, certainly not given how rattled he was."

Steve brought the jeep to a stop. "We never leave man behind."

Steve's words had been quiet, but loud enough for all the gathered men to hear.

"If there's a chance he's still alive, we need to head into the trees and find him. I'm not writing him off until we see his body. Understood?" Before the others could answer, Steve swatted at his neck. Something had been crawling over his skin. Whatever it had been was nothing more than a pile of glop on the palm of his hand at that point. He wiped his hand clean on the side of his pants.

The others stared at him. It was easy to see that not everyone agreed with his decision, but he was in command and there wasn't a bloody lot they could do about it.

At that exact moment, several trees came crashing to the earth on the far right side of the clearing. Through the opening, lumbered a massive, four legged beast with two large horns that grew from the shield shaped bone of its forehead. A third horn sprouted from the tip of its long, snout-like nose.

"What the heck is that?" Henry asked.

"A triceratops," Tank answered in a voice so quiet that even Steve in the driver's seat near him barely heard him.

The huge beast lumbered about, sniffing the air. Its gaze fell upon the jeep and its eyes drew up into slanted slits of anger.

"Oh crap," Steve muttered. "Don't do anything to tick it off and maybe it'll leave us alone."

"No such luck, boss man!" Watson shouted as the triceratops ground the heels of its feet in the dirt, gave a snort, and came charging towards the jeep like some sort of demonic bull.

Steve slammed the gas pedal to the floor. The jeep lurched forward, building speed as it moved. Poor Watson held onto the mounted .50 cal for dear life, barely managing to stay on the jeep.

Henry and Robbins threw themselves out of the beast's path as it bounded passed them. Neither of the two men dared to take a shot at its backside.

Navigating the bumpy ground and the scattered trees that reached for the sky wasn't an easy thing, but Steve was doing his best as he heard Watson open up on the triceratops with the .50 cal. Watson had gotten his footing back and was using the gun to brace himself even as he fired it.

The high-powered round blew holes in the triceratops' armor, but that only seemed to make it angrier. It gave a thunderous roar as it picked up its pace and lowered its head deeper into a ramming position.

Tank was keeping a firm hold on Jones to keep him from sliding out of the jeep as Steve drove on like a madman.

"How fast is that thing?" Steve yelled so he could be heard over the chatter of the .50 cal. "I'm pushing forty five!"

"I don't know," Tank admitted, shouting back at him, "but it's gaining on us!"

Watson was still blazing away at the creature, a stream of automatic fire sparking off its armored head in some places and ripping out bloody holes into its body in others.

Tank leaned over Jones' body, digging around in

the cluttered mess of supplies crammed into the jeep's rear. He yanked a slender, metal tube from the mess and whacked Watson on the leg with it to get the man's attention.

"Use this!" Tank shouted.

Still holding onto the .50 to keep himself from being flung off the jeep's rear, Watson reached down and took the offered weapon. Lowering himself carefully beside the .50, he extended the tube with a sharp clack.

"You're gonna have to brace me!" he shouted at Tank.

Tank planted his feet against the jeep's floor, holding onto Jones with one hand, while his other reached up to steady Watson. The young soldier took aim at the triceratops.

The L.A.W. spat fire as an anti-tank rocket exploded out of it. The rocket flew from the jeep to make contact with the triceratops' head, dead center. The explosion ripped apart its armor and skull alike. The huge beast's now headless form stumbled on for a few more steps and then crashed to the dirt, sliding forward several more yards by its momentum before finally coming to a stop.

"Yee-hah!" Watson whooped.

Steve slowed the jeep and brought it around to head back to where they'd left the others. The back of his hand wiped sweat from his brow as he let out a sigh of relief. That one had been a bit *too* close for his liking.

Robbins and Henry were waiting on them as he brought the jeep to a stop near the area from where Abbott had emerged.

"That was some nice shooting, kid." Tank nodded, looking up at Watson.

Watson beamed at the praise from a veteran like Tank.

"Thank God that's over with," Steve said, his foot still on the brake, as he reached towards the jeep's gearshift to put it in park. He never got the chance though. The creature dropped out of the sky like a jet fighter on a strafing run. The thick, curved claws of its feet crunched into and through the metal of the jeep's sides. In the next second, the jeep was airborne. Steve could hear the other men, still on the ground, firing at the monster as he rolled out of the driver's seat and dropped to the earth below. Tank and Jones had been thrown from the jeep and lay near him. Jones was on top of Tank, writhing about and howling in pain, his already broken leg, twisted completely around sideways despite its splint.

"Watson!" Steve heard Tank cry out from where he lay but the bird-like monster flew away, as quickly as it had swooped in, with Watson's body hanging limply in its blood-smeared beak and the jeep itself being carried along beneath its body by its feet.

"Hold your fire!" Steve shouted, getting to his feet. "That thing is long gone and already out of range!"

Henry and Robbins reluctantly lowered their rifles but their eyes stayed glued on the sky above them.

Tank was struggling to get Jones under control as the smaller man continued to scream and tear at him from the delirious state the pain of his broken leg had driven him. Steve marched over to where the two men wrestled and slammed the butt of his M-16 into the back of Jones' skull. Jones gave a grunt and fell unconscious in Tank's arms.

"Thanks," Tank stammered.

"It had to be done," Steve answered grimly.

"We should leave him," Henry said. "He's only going to get us killed."

Steve spun on Henry, grabbing him by the Kevlar vest he wore, and pulled him close.

"We leave no one, *no one,* behind," Steve growled and then shoved Henry from his feet. Henry landed on his backside, staring up at Steve with an expression that was part anger and part fear.

"Uh, guys," Robbins interrupted. "We're sitting ducks out here, ya know?"

"Tank! You carry Jones. I'll hang back and cover you. Everyone else, double time it for the trees that Abbott came out of!" Steve ordered.

An hour later, the only thing Steve wanted to do was find some shade and collapse in it. His sweat drenched clothes clung to his skin. The heat and the hurried pace he set for the group were taking a toll on everyone. Tank and Robbins had it the worst. Tank looked on the verge of falling over but somehow he kept going with Jones' unconscious body draped over his right shoulder. Robbins carried the group's only remaining .50 caliber and a belt of ammo for it.

The group had been lucky though. So far, they hadn't stumbled into any more of the dinosaurs that called this place home. Steve knew their luck wouldn't hold out forever. They needed desperately to find somewhere to hold up and rest. There were mountains in the distance and Steve hoped that they could find shelter there.

There had been no signs of people or even civilization. Henry had brought along a radio unit salvaged from one of the jeeps. Every time the group took a five-minute break, Henry spent his time fiddling with it and trying to raise anyone he could. All he got was dead air and static for his efforts. It was as if they weren't even on Earth anymore. At least not the Earth they had come from.

Steve had no rational explanation of what had happened to them. Nothing about their current situation made any sense. The last thing any of them remembered was driving into the sand storm with a pack of crazed terrorists on their heels.

Robbins was a science fiction geek and always had been. He theorized that the sand storm hadn't been a natural occurrence, but rather some kind of temporal or dimensional vortex that had swept them up to only God knew where. Tank bought into Robbins' theory hook, line, and sinker. Henry, however didn't. The man was adamant they were still on the same Earth they had been and somewhere in the same region that were when the sand storm hit them. Steve could see both theories having some merit to them, but in truth, all that mattered to him was keeping the others alive and getting them home.

As the sun started its descent and the shadows of

the jungle grew deeper, the group reached the base of a small mountain. Steve allowed Tank and Robbins to take a much-needed break from the group's long march. He and Henry left Jones with them and headed off to get a better look at the area surrounding the mountain. The two of them hadn't gone far at all when they discovered the mouth of a cave leading into the mountain itself.

Henry gestured at the cave. "What ya thinking, boss?'

"I'm thinking we might have just found a place to stay."

"We've got no idea what's in there," Henry pointed out.

"Only one way to find out," Steve answered. He shrugged off the backpacked he carried and dug through it, producing a flare. "If there are more of those creatures in there, this will flush them out."

"You sure that's what we really want to do?" Henry frowned. "Those things aren't exactly easy to kill."

"You got a better plan?" Steve challenged.

When Henry didn't answer, Steve lit the flare and threw it into the cave. It clattered across the cave's rock floor, illuminating the area inside.

"You see anything?" Steve asked, squinting into the light.

"Not a thing," Henry said, looking relieved. "That cave goes must go way back into the mountain though. I can't see the end of it from here."

Steve grunted. "Guess we're gonna have to go in then."

"With respect, sir, you first." Henry's knuckles were white from how tightly he clutched his M-16.

"I don't want to waste any more flares," Steve said. "Help me make some torches."

There was plenty of suitable wood around. Getting the torches cobbled together and lit didn't take them long. Both men held a torch in one hand and a weapon in the other as they entered the cave. Henry kept his M-16 ready for single-handed fire, while Steve slung his, opting to draw his sidearm instead.

The interior of the cave was large and wide. It stretched back a good distance into the side of the mountain but thankfully did finally come to an end. There were no side passages leading into or out of it. It was just one big space. The disturbing part was that someone appeared to have been living in it already. There were crudely made fire pits in several places along the cave floor, a stack of bones in one of its far corners, and scattered animal hides that might have been used as blankets or even clothing everywhere.

"Sir!" Henry barked from the direction he'd wandered off in as Steve had stopped to examine the fire pits. "You need to see this!"

Steve moved to Henry's side as the man held the flames of his torch up next to the cave's wall.

"What in the Hades are those?" Steve asked, staring at the wall.

"Paintings maybe?" Henry shrugged.

"My nine year old can draw better than this," Steve commented, but there was no denying that the scrawled marks on the wall were indeed paintings of some kind.

The section of the paintings that was lit up by the light of Henry's torch showed a group of men, women, and children fleeing a giant shape that walked on two legs.

"You think those people live here?" Henry asked.

"If they did, they aren't here now." Steve shook his head, "And this is the best, okay, the only place we've come across that offers us a defendable position. Let's go get the others, because I don't think we'll be finding anywhere better before nightfall and I sure don't want to be out there with those monsters in the dark."

****

Jones lay by the fire that Steve had built in the center of the cave. The roof of the cave was high and there was enough open space inside that the smoke, while not pleasant, wasn't so dense as to be a danger to them. Jones was still out of it. He would awaken for a moment, raving, only to go back out from the pain he was in. Steve wagered Jones wouldn't hang on for much longer. His leg was a mess and the man had lost a *lot* of blood. If the wound itself didn't get him, infection surely would, given time.

Steve gnawed on a ration bar as he watched Robbins sitting at the entrance of the cave. The group had set up the .50 caliber there in the hope that if anything came at them during the night, Robbins would be able to tear it to pieces before it got inside. Steve knew the man was exhausted but Robbins had volunteered to take the watch saying that he couldn't rest even if he tried.

Henry had no problem getting some rest. The man was sprawled out on the opposite side of the fire from where Jones lay and was already snoring like a buzz saw.

Tank sat near the rear of the cave, nervously puffing on cigarette after cigarette. There was a growing pile of butts on the cave floor next to him. Steve got up and moved to join Tank.

"Easy there, big guy," he warned. "When those run out, you may not be getting any more for a while."

"It's okay," Tank chuckled. "I'm not really a smoker. I took these off Jones."

He held up a half full, blood smeared pack for Steve to see. "Don't reckon Jones will be needing them anyway, sir."

"I hate to admit it," Steve whispered, "but you're likely right there. Doubt he'll make it through the night."

"Figures our medic would be the first to die." Tank ground out the stub of his cigarette and shook a fresh one from the pack. He lit up with a lighter Steve guessed he had taken from Jones too.

"I didn't know Lawrence well but he seemed like a good guy." Steve gestured at the pack Tank held. "Mind if I have one?"

"Here." Tank tossed him the pack and the lighter. "You can have them. I thought smoking was supposed to help calm you down, but these things aren't doing squat."

"Thanks," Steve nodded as he lit up a smoke.

"We got movement!" Robbins yelled from his position at the mouth of the cave.

Steve had barely gotten two drags off his smoke, but he stubbed it out all the same. Both he and Tank grabbed up their rifles and rushed towards Robbins. Steve stared over Robbins' shoulder out into the darkness but he couldn't see anything. The night outside was calm and quiet.

"What did you see?" Steve asked.

"Could've been more of those smaller creatures like the first ones we ran into."

"The Troodons?" Steve asked.

Robbins and Tank both shoot him a confused look.

"What?" Steve grinned. "I loved dinosaurs as a kid, okay?"

"Troodons," Robbins repeated the name. "Yeah, sure, whatever you want to call them. I think that's what I saw."

"Troodons aren't nearly as bad as some of the things that could be out," Steve told them. "Trust me on that one."

"Well, maybe whatever you saw is gone now," Tank said. "I sure don't see anything."

"We'll see. I'm pretty sure that whatever else is out there won't have a problem paying us a visit." Steve tightened his grip on his rifle and stared out into the dark.

The sun had long disappeared, and the sky was filled with stars; more stars than any of the men had seen before. Had they not been pre-occupied with the threat of a dinosaur attack, they would surely have taken the time to appreciate the beauty of the dark sky.

"They won't get me without a fight," Robbins growled and spat onto the floor of the cave. "You guys go get some rest. I've got this." Never once did Robbins take his eyes from the world before him.

Moving back into the rear of the cave, Tank and Steve sat by the fire and stared into the flames. Neither was in the mood to talk. They had too much on their minds. The dancing flames provided a good distraction, while Henry's deep snoring was a reminder that they were still together. They were still alive. As long as that was the case, they would keep fighting.

Steve had no idea what time it was, nor how long they had been in the cave. Tank had joined Henry in a deep sleep. His own rasping snores seemed to make the whole cave vibrate. Steve hadn't slept; not a wink.

Getting to his feet, Steve moved to join Robbins at the cave mouth. He relieved him from duty. No point in the both of them getting no rest.

"Can't sleep?" Robbins asked as Steve moved beside him.

"No."

"Do you really think we will find Lawrence?" Robbins asked, taking his eyes away from the night to look at Steve. The light from the stars was enough to show that Robbins had been crying.

"I hope so, but I think we have bigger issues to worry with now, finding a way to get home for one of them." Steve frowned. "Go get some rest. I'll take over." Without waiting for an answer, Steve slid behind the .50 caliber gun, and settled into place.

The night passed slowly. If there was a moon, it was on the other side of the mountain. Alone, with the others in the back of the cave, Steve finally allowed himself to snap out of the military mindset. He was a soldier, and he was the man in charge, but he was also a family man. He fished into the pocket of his jacket and pulled out a crumpled photograph. His wife and his two children smiled back at him.

"I'll find a way to get us home, guys. I promise," Steve whispered to the picture. He slid it back into this pocket. He adjusted his grip on the machine gun, and said a silent prayer for both him and his family.

Just as it looked as though the night would never end, a golden reddish glow began to light the horizon. Moving away from the gun, trying to waken his stiffened legs, Steve walked towards the back of the cave to wake the others.

"Tank, Robbins, wake up, guys. Dawn is here, and we should look to make an early move." Steve shook the two men, who woke in an instant. Henry woke with a jolt, as if being ripped from slumber. He sat bolt upright and grabbed for his gun.

"Whoa, easy there," Steve called out. Henry looked around, and then to his brothers in arms. His face focused and then dropped.

"I hoped this was the dream," he spoke.

"I know what you mean," Robbins echoed.

"I want to head out early. I figure we head further up the mountain if we can, then we can at least get a better view of the land. Maybe get a better idea of where Lawrence may be headed if he's still alive. He didn't have that much of a head start on us. Grab your things. We move out in fifteen," Steve ordered, slipping out of the mindset he had found while on watch. It was time to be the leader once more. "How's Jones doing, Henry?" Jones and Henry lay on the far side of the fire pit.

"He's... he's gone." Henry reached over and felt his friend's neck for a pulse. The two had known each other well. They had been through boot camp together.

"God speed," Steve said before turning away from the group. "We still leave in fifteen minutes," he called, knowing that there was no time to mourn, much less give the man a proper burial.

They did not have many things to pack, but after grabbing their weapons and stamping out the remains of their fire, the men were ready.

"What about Jones?" Henry asked.

"We can't take him with us," Robbins answered, voicing the opinion they all had, but refused to say.

"He's safer here," Tank said. He bent down to the body, which they had placed on its back, hands folded neatly over each other, and he removed Jones' dog tags. Tank said a prayer for Jones and then got to his feet.

Steve was waiting for them at the mouth of the cave. He was silent, his rifle at the ready. "Be quiet. Something's out there," he whispered as the men approached him.

"What is it?" Tank asked.

"Not sure. I heard it in the night too. Something

rustling over the rocks. There. Look." Steve pointed as two long, moving stalks came into view.

"We need to move. NOW!" Robbins called as the creature emerged. It looked like a cockroach, only it was larger, much larger.

There was no need for further orders. The group burst into a run, and behind them, the creature did the same. Its multitude of legs tapped against the rock surface, and it gave a series of angry clicks.

The men ran from the cave and began a frantic scramble up the mountain. There was a clear passage they followed, but the morning was already warm, and their exertion from the previous day had them all still feeling sluggish.

Turning to face the creature as they moved, Steve fired a burst from his M16, but the shells just embedded themselves in the creature's plated shell.

The creature was close to two meters wide and as long as a bus. Its body was covered in armor plates. Its head was a round ball that stuck out from the foremost plate. Two large black eyes bulged from the front, and two long antennae grew from the blackened flesh.

Steve fired another burst, aiming at the creature's head. One of its eyes exploded in a shower of hot goo, and it gave a scream that sounded chillingly human. The creature stopped its advance, its body thrashing around in pain. Raising itself upward, its segmented body curling up on itself, the creature revealed its fleshy undercarriage. One final burst of gunfire saw the creature fall to the ground, blood oozing from the wounds.

"It's still not dead," Robbins remarked as the

others turned around.

"Don't care," Steve wheezed. His ribs were still sore from the car crash, and running only heightened the stabbing pain.

Regrouped, they moved around the creature and moved around the mountain, wanting to put distance between them and the cave in case there were more of them.

They didn't encounter anything else for the rest of the morning. The biggest threat they faced was exhaustion. The sun rose fast, and the temperature, while cooler than in the trees, was still dangerous.

At Steve's command, the group stopped to rest. Nobody offered any complaints, and when a giant scorpion appeared ahead of them, none made a move to take it down. The creature was a large as a dog, and crossed their path as it traveled around the mountain. Sensing them, it stopped, but soon moved on.

"That thing was huge," Henry said, once it had skittered from view.

"It's a dangerous world out here, man. We don't belong," Tank answered. "We can't stay in the mountain. Lawrence couldn't have made it this far, and we are moving further away from where we need to be to get out of this place."

"If we can get out," Henry added. "What makes you think that is even possible?"

Tank said nothing but looked as if he was on the edge of ripping Henry apart for saying aloud what all of them surely had to be wondering.

"Guys, look at this," Steve's voice silenced both men, who sat staring at each other, with narrowed eyes and clenched jaws. "Is this what I think it is?" He held a long stick in his hands. It had been whittled to a fine point at one end.

"It looks like a stick with a rock tied to it," Robbins offered.

"It looks like a spear," Henry countered. "Let me take a look at it."

"Whatever it was, someone made it," Tank chimed in. "Lawrence?"

"I don't think so. Why would he make a spear? He had an M-16 and his handgun. We would have heard it if he had been this close, and using that much firepower.

"What are you saying?" Tank asked, as he rose and walked to take a closer look at the spear.

"Well, think about it. There was a fire pit in the cave, drawings on the wall, and now this. I... I don't think we are alone here," Steve answered.

The words took a few moments to sink in, but everybody knew what he meant, and what it meant for them.

The mountain they were on was only a small one compared to the rest of the range that towered over them. In spite of that, an hour later, they had reached a height that offered them a better view of their surroundings. The forest was thick, the trees unyielding. It was a carpet of green, for the most part. There was one area of dead trees. A large expanse, far in the distance. Beyond that, the green began again, extending until it met the horizon.

"There, look at that." Robbins pointed at the expanse of death. "That has got to mean something, right?" He asked the group, hopeful.

"Maybe. We need to find Lawrence first. I will not leave here without knowing what happened to him," Steve answered knowing there was little truth to his words but he felt he needed to say them anyway.

"We need to find water," Tank shot back, wiping his sweat soaked brow with the back of his hand. His face was a deep red, not that much darker than its normal shade, but it was a reminder to them all. They needed to think smart. They were in a strange world, but the normal rules still applied.

"There, what's that?" Henry squinted and pointed down the mountainside to a point to the right of the clearing.

The rest of the group looked, following the line of Henry's outstretched arm. Something glinted, glistened among the trees. "It looks like water. A lake or something?" Tank offered.

"I think so," Steve agreed. "Look there, through the trees. I can see a river too."

The others were silent for a while, but then they all saw it; small glistening patches, shining through the thick canopy of trees.

"If Lawrence is alive, he would head for water too." Robbins turned and faced Steve, but there was no time for anybody to answer.

The world above them turned dark, a shadow passed over them, and a whistling sound filled the air. The dinosaur landed on its back with an explosive thud. The ground shook from the force of the impact.

The dinosaur completely blocked the path they been following. Falling from the sky, it would seem, to trap them. The creature gave a series of barked grunts as it rocked from side to side in an attempt to right itself. Its short stubby legs wiggled frantically, but it was no use. The fat armored spines of the creature's shoulders dug into the ground and prevented it from righting itself.

"Where they hell did that come from?" Robbins cried out, more in shock than fear.

"Up there." Tank pointed further up the mountain to a rocky ledge a hundred meters above their head. "There is something else up there too."

"Run," Steve gave the order as a number of heads appeared over the edge of the ledge. The bodies soon followed, and suddenly a pack of smaller, dome-headed dinosaur was bearing down on them.

The group burst into a run, charging past the overturned beast. They propelled themselves down the mountain, abandoning the path, choosing instead a mad, off-road scramble.

They heard the impact as the dinosaurs charged into the overturned beast. The heavy thudding of their full-speed blows were thick and heavy on the air. Nobody turned around, but the groans of pain made it evident that the fight would have a winner soon.

Once down the mountain, a wide-open patch of rocky ground was what they needed to clear before they made it to the trees.

"Head for the trees. We need shelter," Steve wheezed. His lungs were on fire, and his chest was exploding with every step.

Nobody voiced an objection and the four men

sped across the rocky ground. They had not gotten half way before the ground once again began to tremble beneath them. A series of screams went up into the air, and in the blink of an eye, the ground exploded.

Winged creatures took flight, bursting from the ground, their wings the same gray coloration as the ground they had built their nests on.

"Move, move," Steve ordered, as a small pterodactyl swooped down on him. It was no bigger than an owl, and he was able to swat it away with his rifle.

The sky darkened as the group filled the sky. The flap of their wings combined and rolled like thunder.

They were nearing the trees, when Robbins screamed. Steve turned on the run and saw his friend being hoisted from the ground by a large beast, the size of a small car. Steve opened up a burst and bullets tore holes in the creature's wings. It released its grip on Robbins, who fell to the ground landing badly.

He made it to his feet, as gunfire rang out from the others also. Limping, Robbins built up some speed and made it to Steve.

"Where did they come from?" Robbins hissed through the pain.

"This is their nesting ground. We woke them," Steve replied as he swatted away another smaller creature.

To their left, Tank had opened fire on a larger bird, wounding it, and buying himself enough time to make it to the trees. Henry soon followed.

Robbins hobbled into the coverage as third in line, and Steve brought up the rear, sending a sweeping shower of bullets into the creatures. His intention was not to kill, but the ward them off.

"That was close," Tank barely managed to utter.

"It's not over yet," Steve told them. "We need to stay alert. How are we doing on ammo?"

They did a quick check and the results were not great. Steve slid his last clip into his M-16, while Tank and Henry each had one spare. Robbins was already on his last. It didn't help that they had left the .50 caliber beast back at the cave entrance.

"Well, at least it looks like we are heading to the water. Stay alert. We don't know what else is out there," Steve offered.

They moved through the trees in a rough formation. All but Tank had swapped their rifles for handguns. They were caked with sweat and their bodies ached. Yet, they pushed forward. Robbins was limping, but he assured them it was nothing more than a mild sprain. The look on his face told a different story, but Steve did not push.

"What were those things back there, the ones on the mountain?" Henry asked when they stopped to rest. They handed around one canteen of water, careful not to take too much at one time.

"I think the big thing was a panoplosaurus. The others, they were stegoceras, or something like that. I don't remember all the names. I was a kid. I know mostly from helping my son with his science project last year," Steve offered, his voice faltering at the mention of his kids.

"You have kids?" Henry asked.

"Yeah, two." Steve nodded.

"Me too, well, one is still cooking, but I say it counts." Henry smiled at the thought of his baby, and then his face also dropped. "We're never getting back to them, are we?" He was holding back a flood of tears; the tears that only a parent could understand.

"We will. I believe it, and you need to also," Steve said, rising to his feet. "Let's push on. That lake was a long way, a couple of days at least, but the river, we should be able to make this afternoon.

They set off again, unaware of the eyes that were following them through the jungle.

****

The group found water around midday. What they had seen from the mountains turned out to be a small lake. Its water was crisp and clear. Robbins hobbled to the lake's edge and dropped down on all fours, splashing his head into it. When he jerked it back up, he shook his soaked hair flinging water.

"Sweet goodness!" Robbins smiled. "That feels good. Don't taste bad either."

"You idiot," Henry raged. "Who knows what you've just exposed yourself to?"

"Cool it!" Steve snapped taking charge of the situation. "Henry is right, Robbins. We have the gear to check it, at least somewhat. This whole place is a nightmare. We need to keep our heads and be careful."

Robbins stretched out on the bank next to the

lake. "Tasted fine to me," he said again with a grin.

"Henry, test the water. Make sure it's safe," Steve ordered. "Tank, keep an eye on the trees around us. We don't want any unexpected company. I think we've had more than our fair share of that already since we ended up in this place."

"Yes sir!" the two men chorused and then set about their tasks.

Steve sat down next to Robbins. "You sure that leg is okay?"

"I'm fine," Robbins grunted, annoyed though he understood Steve's concern.

"You landed on it pretty hard."

"Not that bad," Robbins admitted. "Truth is something bit me in the cave last night. Biggest dang bug I'd ever seen until that big freaking thing came at us this morning."

Steve frowned. "Why didn't you tell me?"

"Ain't nothing to be worried about, sir," Robbins told him. "And you sure got more to worry about than my leg."

"Water's fine!" Henry announced. He started systematically filling up the group's canteen for them, one by one.

Tank was already wading into it, splashing it up over his arms and chest. "Robbins was right!" he shouted. "It feels great too!"

A buzzing noise, as loud as a helicopter, came from the other side of the lake.

"Oh, for the love of. . ." Tank rasped. "What now?"

Robbins, Henry, and Steve saw the thing coming as it zeroed in on Tank and skimmed the surface of the water towards him. The thing looked like a dragonfly on steroids. All three of them leaped to their feet.

"Hold your fire!" Steve warned. The giant insect was already too close to Tank for them to take a shot at it without risking hitting him too.

Startled, Tank turned around just in time to look straight into the dragonfly's watermelon sized eyes before it plowed into him. It knocked him aside as if he was nothing. Tank flopped sideways into the water and vanished beneath it as the dragonfly flew onward towards the bank.

With Tank out of the way, Steve yelled, "Take the thing out!"

Henry and Robbins opened up with their pistols as Steve unslung his M-16. Thankfully, he didn't need to use it. The insect proved an easy killed. It took less than half dozen well aimed shots from his men to send it spiraling into the water at the lake's edge. It crashed there with a huge splash and it didn't move again.

"Tank!" Henry yelled and started to jump into the lake after the big man.

Steve grabbed him. "No!"

Tank had yet to come up out of the water and there was no sign of him.

"We've got to help him!" Henry shook free of Steve's hold. He froze though as the water exploded. Out of it rose a head so large it chilled Steve to his very bones. The head sat atop a snake like body or neck that stretched several yards in length, before its bottom was obscured by the water.

"Is that thing a snake?" Henry muttered, apparently in shock.

Steve shoved him ahead of himself as he shouted, "Run!"

Henry didn't have to be told twice. He took off, sprinting into the trees.

Steve paused to help Robbins up, and he half dragged him along as they both followed after Henry.

The monster behind them loosed a roar that seemed to shake the very ground under their feet, but it didn't come after them. Steve looked over his shoulder to see the thing's massive head plunge under the water once more.

After a few minutes, the three men collapsed in the shade of the trees, exhausted. Their breath came in ragged pants.

"This crap is really getting old," Robbins complained.

"Tell me about it," Steve sympathized.

Henry was sobbing where he lay. "Tank," he mumbled his friend's name over and over.

"And then there were three," Robbins said coldly.

Anger flared inside Steve at Robbins' words. He held it in though. Losing it now wasn't going to help anybody.

"I'm sorry," Steve forced the words to come out in a calm, level tone.

"You're sorry?" Henry demanded, sitting up. "You should be! This all your fault!"

"Whoa," Robbins cautioned the smaller man as Henry brought the barrel of his pistol up at Steve.

"This is all your fault, sir," Henry spat the last word as an insult.

"How do you figure that?" Robbins challenged Henry, getting his attention in the process.

Henry whipped his pistol around to aim at Robbins. "How is it not? If he hadn't. . ."

"If he hadn't saved us all when the crap hit the fan back at base camp? If he hadn't risked his neck over and over to keep us all alive here?" Robbins pointed out. "Truth is we would all already be dead without him."

Steve remained silent during the whole exchange, watching Henry closely. It was as if Henry had forgotten the two of them were armed too. He could have taken Henry out with his sidearm at any time, knowing he was faster, but wanted to give Henry a chance to back down before it came to that.

Robbins' words must have gotten through to Henry. He lowered his pistol, looking ashamed.

"I'm sorry," Henry sobbed, tears streaming over his cheeks. He tossed his pistol aside. "I'm sorry."

"It's okay," Steve assured him. "This place...it's getting to us."

Steve retrieved Henry's pistol and handed it back to him. "The only hope we have is sticking together."

"I think it's time to admit that Lawrence is dead," Robbins said.

"Agreed," Steve nodded. "Our focus needs to

be on getting home."

"The radio we left in the cave is our best shot of that," Henry said, wiping away his tears and seeming to pull himself together. "You saw how far this jungle goes in *every* direction. With all the monsters in this place, we're never going be able to walk out of here. If we can use the radio, maybe get through to someone somehow, we can call for an evac."

"Gotta say that sounds like as good a plan as anything I can come up with." Robbins looked to Steve.

"Okay then," Steve said. "Then I guess that's what we need to try for. You said you weren't able to get anyone on it though, Henry."

Henry rubbed at his cheeks with the fingers of his right hand. "Yeah, but maybe there's just something here messing with the signal. If we take it higher, maybe further up in the mountains, we might be able to get one out to the real world."

Steve nodded again. *The real world,* he thought. *I suppose that's as good a thing as any to call home.*

"Let's get moving then," Steve ordered. He shot a glance at Robbins who was having trouble getting to his feet. "And if that leg of yours isn't any better by the time we get back to cave, you're letting me take a look at it, even if I have to knock you on your butt to do it. Understood?"

"Yes sir," Robbins growled, reluctantly.

****

Robbins' condition had gotten terribly worse by the time they reached the cave. Steve had nearly carried him the last few klicks, supporting most of his weight on himself. It was more than just the pain in his leg. They had been forced to stop several times for Robbins to be violently sick. How the man had as much inside him to vomit up onto the jungle floor as he did, Steve had no idea. Robbins had somehow managed to become pale despite the heat and blazing sun that had burnt down on them most of the day. More than that, it had taken on a greenish hue.

What worried Steve the most was Robbins' eyes. The man's very pupils seemed to be melting and reshaping themselves, the white of his eyes around them becoming a sickly yellow. Steve had never even heard tell of anything like what was happening to Robbins. His best guess was that the bite Robbins had gotten in the cave had been poisonous and maybe his liver was failing from it. He remembered something about yellow and liver failure from school but not enough for to say for certain that was what was actually happening.

Henry had pulled ahead of them. Steve agreeing to follow his lead with the radio had given Henry real hope of making it home again. None of them had talked about the chance that they weren't even on Earth anymore, not really, but Steve knew Henry believed deeply that they were.

Entering the cave ahead of them at a hurried pace and rather recklessly by the way Steve saw things, Henry vanished inside it.

"Holy!" Henry cried out.

Steve eased Robbins to the ground. Robbins was mostly out of it. Steve doubted the man was even aware of the world around him. His skin was hot to the touch and slicked with a cold sweat. Steve knew it wasn't just from the heat. As soon as he had Robbins safely put down, he raced after Henry, taking comfort in the fact that he hadn't heard any gunfire from within the cave...yet.

He found Henry kneeling next to the .50 caliber. The large weapon was a mess. Something or someone looked to have hammered it with a rock until it was dented and nearly in pieces.

Henry spun on him. "What the heck happened to this?"

"No idea," Steve said.

As if suddenly remembering why they had come back to the cave, "The radio!" Henry blurted out and ran towards the rear of the cave where they had left it.

Steve though headed for the fire pit in the center of the cave where Jones' body lay. Henry had paused to fire up a torch, and in its light, Steve saw what was left of Jones. Something had torn open his chest. Jagged bits of his ripped open ribcage stuck upwards into the air where they had been folded outward. Steve gagged from the sight of it. The smell of Jones' rotting flesh didn't help any either. Jones' clothes were gone along with his skin. His eyes were nothing more than empty cavities. Whatever had done this to him couldn't have been an animal. There was far too much precision and skill in how the man's skin had been removed. Chunks of meat were missing in various spots from his corpse too. They seemed to have been sawed away with something akin to a primitive knife. Steve recalled the spear tip they had found and a shudder ran through him.

"Henry," he called quietly.

Henry didn't answer him. Steve looked toward the light of Henry's torch to see him kneeling over the smashed remains of the group's radio they had looted from one of the jeeps.

"Henry," Steve called quietly again. "We need to go."

"It's smashed, Steve," Henry whimpered without taking his eyes off the broken radio, "too bad for me to fix it."

"We can go back to the jeeps and get another, Henry," Steve whispered, "But we need to go *now!*"

"What's the point?" Henry asked finally turning towards Steve. There were fresh tears in his eyes. "Even if we make it back to the jeeps *and* there's still another radio that works there, we're never getting out of this place."

"Come on, Henry," Steve urged. "We don't have time for this right now."

A violent hiss tore Steve's attention towards the mouth of the cave. Robbins was standing there, the light of the sun outside silhouetting his figure. Steve blinked and stared at Robbins. The man was moving as he was perfectly fine, maybe better than fine. Robbins eyes glowed yellow in the shadows just inside the cave as he stepped towards Steve.

Robbins' tongue lolled out from between his lips. Only it wasn't a human tongue anymore. It was long and forked. It flicked at the air as if tasting it before disappearing into Robbins mouth once more.

Steve leveled his M-16 at Robbins' chest. "Stay right where you are, man," Steve warned.

A trio of pistol cracks echoed in the cave as the barrel of Henry's pistol barked fire. The rounds from it struck Robbins and sent him staggering back out of the cave into the light of the sun. His skin was covered in scales that appeared to be growing *over* his flesh and replacing it.

"Kill it, Steve!" Henry shouted. "That thing isn't Robbins anymore!"

The thing that had been Robbins righted itself and came lumbering forward. Its lips parted to show fang like teeth in a savage snarl.

Steve hesitated, his mind reeling. Robbins started for him but stumbled, giving a loud grunt of pain, and toppled to the cave floor with a spear buried in his back.

Two women and a man dressed in tattered rags appeared in the mouth of the cave.

"Come on!" one of the women screamed, motioning for Steve and Henry to follow her. "They know we're here! They will be more of them coming!"

"People!" Henry exclaimed like an idiot, his eyes going wide.

"Yeah, we're people!" the man shouted, "Now, move it!"

Steve and Henry sprinted after the trio, doing their best to keep up with them, as they fled the cave, leaving the shattered radio and everything else inside it behind them.

****

The trio moved fast and silent over the rocks, their bare feet not slowing their progress. To the contrary, Henry and Steve struggled to keep up, their heavy military gear and cumbersome boots made the climb even more tiring.

"Get rid of all this," one of the women spoke. The trio had stopped moving to allow the others to catch up. She pulled on Steve's Kevlar vest and kicked his boots. "We can't waste time. They are coming for us." As she spoke, Steve noticed that she never stopped scanning. All three of them. Their eyes were permanently on the move, scanning for any sign of danger.

"Who are you?" Steve asked, but a raised hand from the male in the group silenced him.

"There is no time. Come with us, now. Lose those jackets, keep the boots, and keep quiet. Those weapons of yours will be the death of us all if you fire them," he snapped. The women at least had a friendly tone to their orders, while the man was strictly business. Steve didn't like him.

"You move, and we will follow," Henry interrupted, looking over his shoulder just in time to see the three figures moving up the same path they were following.

They moved as fast as they could, but it was not fast enough. Their pursuers caught up with them, moving over the jagged rocks as well as the smooth path with the greatest of ease. Their hissed breaths sent chills up Steve's spine.

Turning, he pulled his handgun and fired into the chest of the closest creatures. They looked like men; only their skin was dry and scaled. Their skin had a strange, yellow pigmentation, the color of pus.

The bullet tore through the creature's flesh, and a dark red blood spilled from the wound. The bullet's impact made the lizard man stumble, but it didn't stop him.

"Enough with the guns. Three of them are nothing compared to the others the noise will attract," The man roared from up ahead. Steve turned back the way he was going and ran for all he was worth, slipping out of his Kevlar vest as he did.

A whistling sound cut through the air. Steve looked up and ducked just as a large rock came hurtling towards him. It collided with the injured lizard creature and sent it sprawling to the floor. It lay still, but not dead. Steve was sure of that, but it was surely stunned.

"Up here," one of the female voices called. She had thick, southern accent, which caught Henry's attention. He veered to the right, and began to climb up the rocks to where the woman stood.

Steve looked to his left and saw the other woman standing on the other side of the path. Following Henry's lead, Steve veered from his course and began climbing up the rock. The remaining two lizard people were on them, climbing up the rocks behind them, moving vertically as if it was the most natural direction.

Another whistling sound came as each woman

loosed a spear. They found their mark at the first
time of asking. A wet squelching sound signified
the creatures end. Steve glanced over his shoulder
and saw both creatures falling to the floor, their
heads speared through. They landed on the floor in
a heap, blood leaking from their splattered bodies.

"What were those things?" Steve asked. The
five of them stood together further up the
mountain. He drank greedily from his canteen. His
head pounded from the incessant heat, and his ears
rang from the altitude they had reached.

"They don't have a name, not really. They are
what we are all trying to avoid," the man, who had
yet to introduce himself, snapped in response.

"Robbins, he became one of those things,"
Henry stammered. He still wore his vest, which
was stained with vomit from where he had
collapsed and brought their group a halt on the
mountainside.

"The bite."

"Bite?"

"He was bitten last night in the cave. He told me
down by the lake. I don't know what it was..."
Steve began to answer, taking another deep draw
from his canteen mid-sentence.

"It doesn't matter what it is. You get bit by
anything out here, you become one of those things.
One of the Lizards," the man offered in brief
explanation. "I bet you thought the worst things out
here were the dinosaurs, didn't you," he scoffed.

"Don't mind Ray, he's a grump, doesn't like
meeting new people," One of the women, a
brunette with bright green eyes spoke. "My name is

Nancy, that's Ray, and that there is Sarah-Jayne."

"What is this place?" Steve asked, shaking the offered hand. He offered his own to Ray, who made no move to reciprocate.

"It's hell. It's home. It doesn't matter. We are here now, and all you need to think about is staying alive. We won't save your ass again," Ray snarled once again.

"You are military too, Ray?" Steve asked, recognizing the mannerisms in the man.

"Yes, sir. You can call me Master Sergeant if it makes you feel any better. It won't make me like you anymore, but hey, I guess it's still a free world."

"How long have you been here?" Steve asked.

"Time doesn't mean anything here. We... I don't know how to explain it, aging, the passage of time. It's all gone. You are either alive or you are dead," Nancy answered, her more personable character coming to ease the tension that was beginning to grow among them.

"So you mean we won't get any older?" Henry sat upright, his mind thrown into a fresh loop.

"Exactly. It was nineteen fifty-nine when I arrived. Ray has been here since nineteen forty-two. We have others who have been here even longer than that." Nancy stopped talking, catching her words. She stood up and walked to the edge of the cliff. Looking down, she gave a sigh. "There are more down there. We should get moving." She looked at the two newcomers. "You really should lose that heavy gear. Those guns too... I've never seen anything like them, but they

47

won't help you much out here. That's how we found you…"

"That's also how they found you. Drop those fancy guns, and get moving. We have a lot of ground to cover, and you don't want to be out in the open once night falls." Ray took charge once again. He started walking immediately, not waiting for them or the women.

"Stay quiet. Those things are lightning fast once they catch a scent," Sarah-Jayne said as she followed Nancy and Ray up the mountain. It was the last thing she would ever say.

Steve and Henry dropped their rifles and shed as many clothes as they could before the others got too far ahead of them.

The climb was more of a hike. The terrain underfoot was stable and offered little in the way of natural peril. Yet, the pace they kept was exhausting.

Steve and Henry lagged behind, too far to bother with communication. Their pace was slow, and their breathing was labored, while the others continued on, immune to the conditions.

"Do you believe they have been here for sixty-odd years?" Henry wheezed, taking a drink from his canteen. While their pace had slowed, both men refused to stop.

"I don't know what I believe anymore," Steve answered. He sounded like a man who had lost hope.

"Wait, what's that?" Steve pointed ahead.

"It's them. Something's happened." Henry burst into a run, as both men saw one of the women tumble and fall down the mountain. She tumbled uncontrollably. A cry carried on the wind, and a high-pitched roar like that of a cornered cat followed soon after.

By the time the men reached Sarah-Jayne's body, they knew it was too late. Her face had been torn to shreds, thick stands of skin and hair hung from her skull. Blood obscured her looks and her body was torn and battered from her descent. Her shoulders were both dislocated and her lower leg was broken, the bone protruding through the mangled mess of skin and bubbling blood.

"Her neck is broke," Henry remarked as he bent down to check for a pulse. "Good thing too." He added, rising to his feet.

"What's up there?" He looked over to Steve, who shrugged his shoulders.

They set off together, knowing that it was a case of fight or die. For the two, combat was combat. Once the challenge was laid, everything else fell to one side. Fatigue and injuries were forgotten. They had a target, and they would meet it head on.

They reached the spot where Sarah-Jayne had fallen; the ground was awash with blood. Deep clawed gouges scarred the ground. The sounds of a fight came from behind a rocky outcrop. They moved into the attack, and then it appeared. A giant mountain cat, its fur was thick and yellow. Its long tail coiled and uncoiled in anger. Its head was caked in blood, and large drooping fangs descended from its upper jaw.

A rock was launched from out of sight, and it hit the creature in the face. It shook it off, giving an angry hiss.

"Hey, hey, over here," Steve called, jumping up and down, waving his arms in the air.

"What are you doing?" Henry asked.

"Throw your knife," Steve spoke through a gritted jaw. He didn't have time to offer a more detailed explanation, because the beast was on him.

Slinking low over the ground, stalking its new prey, it moved in for the kill. That was when the knife jammed into its throat, the blade burying itself to the hilt. Blood dribbled from the wound and the large car stumbled. Its front legs buckled, and it fell to its knees. Lunging forward, Steve unsheathed his own blade and in a swift action, slit the beast's throat, showering the ground with blood.

"You crazy son of a gun," Henry exclaimed, slapping Steve on the back. He tugged twice to free his knife from the felled creature's thick, muscular neck.

"You saved us,Nancy spoke, emerging from over the rocks. "Thank you." She smiled.

"Not bad at all." Ray nodded, looking at the dead animal. In that moment, as he looked from it to the two men, something in him changed. His face, his demeanor, it all softened. "Those things are never far from the lizard folk. They keep them like pets. We need to keep moving," he ordered once more, but the hatred had fallen from his tone.

* * *

They climbed in silence, no longer two groups, but one. Ray kept the lead, but he knew the way, and both Steve and Henry were happy to follow. Other than the cat, they had not seen a pre-historic monster since they left the woods. They were beginning to realize what Ray had meant when he said the dinosaurs were the least of their problems.

The mountain was filled with insects and bugs. The scorpion they had seen earlier was nothing compared to the larger specimens they had seen since. They were at least a meter long, with their tails curled. Spiders as large as dinner plates and all manner of bugs and snakes made every step a danger. They understood why their new friends never stopped looking around. If one bite was all it took to turn, death really lurked under every stone.

They reached a cave, just as the heat of the day was reaching its peak. Even without their vests and heavier gear, Henry and Steve were exhausted. Every step was an excruciating experience.

"We will rest here. The sun goes down quickly in this world and we don't want to be caught unawares."

"Is it safe?" Steve asked, peering into the cave's mouth. The darkness within was total. He shuddered, imagining he was staring into the hungry mouth of another beast intent on devouring them.

"It's safe. We have a number of caves cleared out. We found escape routes in most of them too," Nancy answered. "Come on. You guys need to rest. We have some supplies with us, food. Nothing much, but it is good for energy."

Following her, they walked into the darkness. Ray had gone on ahead, a makeshift knife at the ready. They heard him fumbling in the darkness, but before they could ask what he was doing, flames appeared. The heat was not welcome, but the light was invaluable.

Steve and Henry collapsed with their backs against the cave wall. They looked around and saw much the same as in their first cave they had found. The walls were covered in all manner of strange markings. Drawings if would seem. Rudimentary at best in their design.

"Those drawings. What do they mean?" Steve asked as he drank from his canteen. It was almost empty again. His stomach cramped a little, but he didn't care.

"We don't know for sure. They were here long before any of us," Nancy offered. She was sitting on the opposite side of the cave, her legs outstretched. She looked, for all intents and purposes, to be relaxed.

"We figure they are some sort of communication system. Some are clearly maps of the area, and others, well, it's often a guess but some are warnings. Certain creatures live in certain caves. There is an order to the mountains," she continued, looking over at Ray, who had returned from the cave mouth.

"I don't see any of them. I think we are safe," he spoke to Nancy before turning his attention to the others. "What year are you from?" He asked, eying them slowly.

"Twenty-Fifteen," Steve answered. "Rangers, seventy-fifth regiment," he offered, staring at Ray.

"Rangers? Huh." His face lightened once again.

"I was a Ranger. One of the first back in the forties." He offered a smile. "Figured when I saw you that you were from the future, so to speak." He sat beside Nancy and pulled a small, battered tin from his pocket. He opened it and pulled out what looked to be a cigarette. "You guys want one? Not like the smokes you're used to, I'm sure, but it is all we got out here.

Both men graciously declined the smoke. Ray lit his own on the fire, and soon a strange peaty smell was wafting its way around the cave.

"You were in the war?" Steve asked,

"Yeah, I was in Europe. We saw a German unit and were advancing to make contact with them, when suddenly…" Ray stopped talking, searching for the right words, "…the lights went out, and we were here."

"How many of you?"

"Must have been at least fifty. I'm the only one left. Well, only one left alive. There's plenty of them lizard folk out there that were men when they arrived," Ray spoke open and honest.

"Did you ever look for a way out?" Henry asked without thinking.

"Of course we did, genius. There ain't one. In this world, it's not part of the one we know. We are trapped here. You can join us, live together. We hunt, we live. It's not fancy. It's dirty and certainly not easy, but it is better than the alternative," Ray offered. He rose and walked toward Steve.

Understanding the man's intentions, Steve also rose to his feet. They met, and Ray extended his hand. Steve took it in his own, and a bond was formed.

"We will stay here tonight, rest and be ready for the morning. It will be a long hike for you to get to our camp. You two take a watch together now. Nancy and I will do the night. You need to rest," Ray ordered.

There was no argument and no discussion. The decisions were final. Steve and Henry moved to the mouth of the cave, which was deeper than the one lower down the mountain. Sitting together, unarmed in dangerous, unfamiliar surroundings put them both on edge.

"Do you think we can trust them?" Henry asked under his breath.

"Yes," Steve answered. He was lost in thought, staring out over the world. He had the photo of his family in his hands.

Ray was right. The light fell fast. They watched the darkness creeping towards them, tracking its progress as it consumed everything in its path. Ray and Nancy were good to their word. Darkness fell and they appeared in the mouth of the cave.

"Time to change the guard," she said with a smile.

Steve and Henry headed into the back. The temperature had cooled, and the warmth of the fire was a welcome feeling. They settled down and were both asleep within minutes. Dawn brought with it another early start, and a long trek, but with their newfound allies, Steve was able to cast aside the dark thoughts and focus on the silver lining. They were still alive.

***

Their final hike was a surprise, because they never left the cave. Instead, they headed deeper into the dark, each carrying a burning torch to light their way.

"We should ask them about Lawrence," Henry whispered as they walked. In the rush of the previous day, thoughts of Lawrence had slipped through the cracks.

"Is he a friend of yours?" Nancy answered, turning around to look at the men. "Even a whisper travels a long way in these tunnels. They are designed that way. It makes it harder to be ambushed when you hear it coming." She smiled.

"Yes, he was in our group, but... well, we got separated," Steve offered.

Nancy fell silent and slowed her pace. "We didn't want to say anything. We found someone, but he was hurt." In the torchlight, the men could see the pensive look on Nancy's face.

"It's okay. You can be honest with us," Steve coaxed. "We had all but given up hope of finding him alive in this place."

Ahead of them, Ray had also stopped. "You never leave a man behind," he muttered, looking back at them.

"Exactly." Steve nodded.

"He was hurt. He took a nasty fall. He was still unconscious when we left to find you two. Prepare yourselves, because there is a good chance he won't have made it through the night." Ray looked at them, and Steve saw the tired look in his eyes. Long shadows danced over his face, and certainly added to the forlorn look, but Steve knew what the man was feeling.

They started walking again, and by the time light loomed on the horizon, an air of camaraderie had fallen over the group. Nancy had filled the men in on the size of their camp. Twelve people in all. They had, at one point been over fifty strong. A mistake during a hunting trip had seen twelve people killed when they were caught between two ticked off triceratops. Fleeing to the water, they were picked off by a bus-sized crocodile creature.

Ray educated them on the rules of the world. Bites and stings whether fatal or not, tended to result in the emergence of the lizard gene. Nobody knew what caused it, as they had yet to come into contact with any real lizards. They lived in the mountains and hunted the smaller beasts that lived there. The thick jungle was to be avoided. Ever since their hunting accident, contact with the dinosaurs had been reduced.

"We tend to stick to the southern side of the mountains where we just were. That seems to be the safest sector," Ray talked to them without turning around.

Steve and Henry looked at one another. After everything they had experienced since arriving, the notion of that being the safe zone was somewhat troubling.

"Safer?" Henry couldn't help but repeat the word.

"You will see for yourself," Ray answered, pointing to the cave's exit. It loomed ahead of them. The sight spurred them on, their pace quickening.

They emerged on the other side of the mountain. The exit brought them out behind a large patch of rocks, a man-made structure, the purpose of which was clear. It provided shelter to those coming through the tunnel and gave them a chance, should anything be waiting for them.

"The camp is just round here. Ray and I will go first and introduce you to them all. Don't worry. They are an easy going bunch," Nancy explained. "Wait here. I'll come get you."

Steve and Henry did as instructed. Nancy and Ray disappeared from view. The men waited, but when a cry went up, and the chillingly familiar predatory hiss followed it, they had no choice but to move.

The camp was larger than they thought. Makeshift tents had been constructed and there were two stone pillars that marked the entrance. One large fire pit was in the center, with a spit erected over the pit. Hides lay stretched out over the mountain face, drying in the sun, and a pile of bones had been neatly stacked beneath them.

Steve's eager eye found Lawrence, who was lying on the floor, his chest ripped open and his organs devoured. The lizard creature responsible for it was one a several in the camp. It's blood smeared face was a giveaway to his guilt.

"What the…" Henry began, but all eyes turned on them. Cold, yellow eyes stared at them. Forked tongues licked at the air, tasting them.

There was nobody left alive in the camp. Bodies littered the floor. The stench of blood was heavy on the wind, and still the creatures were not satisfied.

"We have to run. Move now!" Nancy screamed, grabbing Ray by the arm.

"It's no use. They are too fast for us," Ray growled. "There's no running from this fight." He spoke, and turned to look at Steve. "Good thing I have some reinforcements." He shot them a strangely timid smile, and Steve knew.

"Where?" He asked.

"The rock, behind you. The one with the cross carved into it. Push it away. You'll see," Ray instructed, as he threw a large stone at the advancing lizard creature.

They had the advantage in height, the camp being below them, at the end of a slope that dropped around three meters. The lizard creatures were smart. They were killers. They had no rush, and so moved slowly, stalking their prey.

Steve pushed against the rock, shoving with all his might. It moved slowly. "Henry, help me." He grunted, and together they pushed the large stone free and revealed Ray's secret cache of weaponry.

"You have this, but we needed to lose our M-16s," Henry began, but Steve silenced him.

"Not the time, Henry, now move," Steve ordered. Reaching into the hollow, his eyes fell instantly on the item he needed.

Steve stood and looked at Ray. "Do it," the older man instructed, his face pensive.

The grenade was old, and there was no way to know if it would detonate. Steve pulled the pin and tightened his grip. Waiting for a slow count, as the lizard creatures gathered to move in for the kill. He threw the grenade and all four of them hit the floor.

The explosion was loud and the shower of debris that fell around them included globs of sizzling lizard flesh.

Getting to their feet, the group looked at the camp, or at what was left of it. The bodies of the lizard people lay scattered over the ground. Nothing had survived.

"What do we do now?" Nancy asked.

For a while, nobody gave an answer. It was then that Steve turned around and looked out over the mountain. He understood then why Ray had called the other side safe. The world that lay before them was no jungle. It was a world of its own. Wide open plains, giant lakes and rivers, thick expanses of jungle scattered amongst it all, and a giant volcano that lay smouldering in the distance. Grey smoke wafting from its mouth. Amongst it all, Steve saw the dinosaurs. Not just one or two, as they had seen before, but herds of them. Everywhere he looked, he could pick out numerous creatures.

"Now," he spoke, standing up straight. "Now, we find our way home." Steve's resolve was clear.

"I told you, there is no escape. We wouldn't last ten minutes down there," Ray answered.

"We've not been doing much better up here. Besides, what is that?" He asked, pointing to his left, where an enormous black obelisk rose from the ground. It grew from within the trees, and stood far taller than anything else in the world.

"Nobody knows. It's always been there. Like I said, we would never reach it," Ray stated again, but even he could not match the power of Steve's stubborn nature.

"Well, I'd rather die trying, than hiding up here. What do you say, Master Sergeant? One last hurrah?" Steve held out his hand, and waited. Ray eyed him up and down, before stepping in and grabbing Steve's hand within his own.

The End

Printed in Great Britain
by Amazon

58592292R00038